EASTER
Coloring Book

This Book Belongs to:

_____

HELLO and WELCOME to

Easter Coloring

by Blue Jewel Books

HAVE A SUPER FUN TIME!

We create our books with great love and care yet mistakes beyond our control can happen in printing, binding and shipping. If you have any questions, comments, concerns, or problems with this book please contact us at: bluejewelbooks@gmail.com.

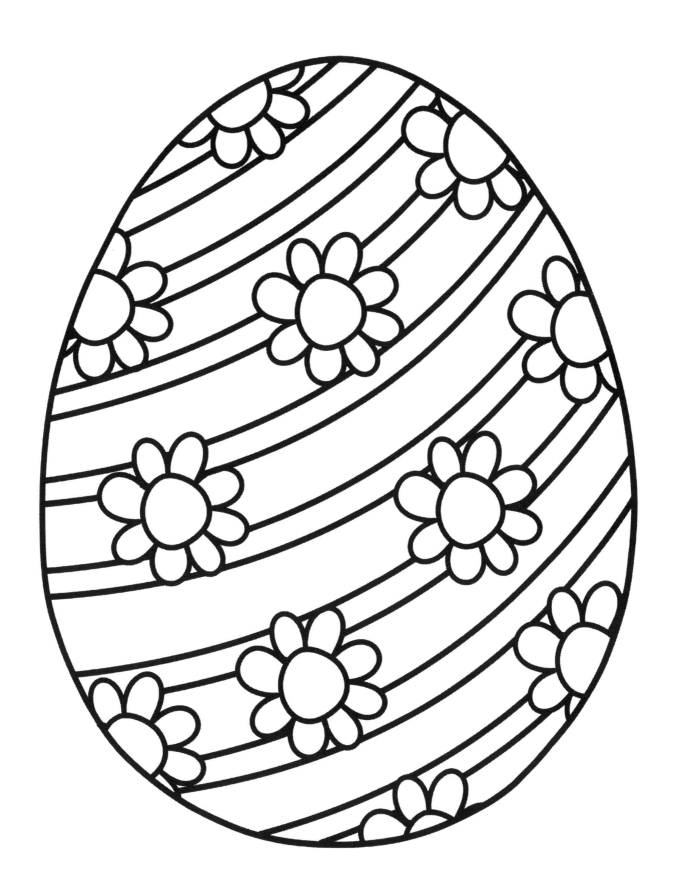

Made in United States
Troutdale, OR
02/25/2024

17966845R00060